The Headswoman

The Headswoman
Kenneth Grahame

MINT EDITIONS

The Headswoman was first published in 1898.

This edition published by Mint Editions 2020.

ISBN 9781513280196 | E-ISBN 9781513285214

Published by Mint Editions®

 MINT
EDITIONS

minteditionbooks.com

Publishing Director: Jennifer Newens
Design & Production: Rachel Lopez Metzger
Project Manager: Micaela Clark
Typesetting: Westchester Publishing Services

Contents

I

I t was a bland, sunny morning of a mediæval May,—an old-style May of the most typical quality; and the Council of the little town of St. Radegonde were assembled, as was their wont at that hour, in the picturesque upper chamber of the Hôtel de Ville, for the dispatch of the usual municipal business. Though the date was early sixteenth century, the members of this particular town-council possessed considerable resemblance to those of similar assemblies in the seventeenth, eighteenth, and even the nineteenth centuries, in a general absence of any characteristic at all—unless a pervading hopeless insignificance can be considered as such. All the character in the room, indeed, seemed to be concentrated in the girl who stood before the table, erect, yet at her ease, facing the members in general and Mr. Mayor in particular; a delicate-handed, handsome girl of some eighteen summers, whose tall, supple figure was well set off by the quiet, though tasteful mourning in which she was clad.

"Well, gentlemen," the Mayor was saying, "this little business appears to be—er—quite in order, and it only remains for me to—er—review the facts. You are aware that the town has lately had the misfortune to lose its executioner,—a gentleman who, I may say, performed the duties of his office with neatness and dispatch, and gave the fullest satisfaction to all with whom he—er—came in contact. But the Council has already, in a vote of condolence, expressed its sense of the—er—striking qualities of the deceased. You are doubtless also aware that the office is hereditary, being secured to a particular family in this town, so long as any one of its members is ready and willing to take it up. The deed lies before me, and appears to be—er—quite in order. It is true that on this occasion the Council might have been called upon to consider and examine the title of the claimant, the late lamented official having only left a daughter,—she who now stands before you; but I am happy to say that Jeanne—the young lady in question—with what I am bound to call great good-feeling on her part, has saved us all trouble in that respect, by formally applying for the family post, with all its—er—duties, privileges, and emoluments; and her application appears to be—er—quite in order. There is, therefore, under the circumstances, nothing left for us to do but to declare the said applicant duly elected. I would wish, however, before I—er—sit down, to make it quite clear to the—er—fair petitioner, that if a laudable desire to save the Council trouble in the matter has led her to a—er—hasty conclusion, it is quite open to her to reconsider her position. Should she determine not to press her claim, the succession to the post would then apparently devolve upon her cousin Enguerrand, well known to you all as a practising advocate in the courts of this town. Though the youth has not, I admit, up to now proved a conspicuous success in the profession he has chosen, still there is no reason why a bad lawyer should not make an excellent executioner; and in view of the close friendship—may I even say attachment?—existing between the cousins, it is possible that this young lady may, in due course, practically enjoy the solid emoluments of the position without the necessity of discharging its (to some girls) uncongenial duties. And so, though not the rose herself, she would still be—er—near the rose!" And the Mayor resumed his seat, chuckling over his little pleasantry, which the keener wits of the Council proceeded to explain at length to the more obtuse.

"Permit me, Mr. Mayor," said the girl quietly, "first to thank you for what was evidently the outcome of a kindly though misdirected feeling on your part; and then to set you right as to the grounds of my application for the post to which you admit my hereditary claim. As to my cousin, your conjecture as to the feeling between us is greatly exaggerated; and I may further say at once, from my knowledge of his character, that he is little qualified either to adorn or to dignify an important position such as this. A man who has achieved such indifferent success in a minor and less exacting walk of life, is hardly likely to shine in an occupation demanding punctuality, concentration, judgment,—all the qualities, in fine, that go to make a good business man. But this is beside the question. My motive, gentlemen, in demanding what is my due, is a simple and (I trust) an honest one, and I desire that there should be no misunderstanding. It is my wish to be dependent on no one. I am both willing and able to work, and I only ask for what is the common right of humanity,—admission to the labour market. How many poor, toiling women would simply jump at a chance like this which fortune, by the accident of birth, lays open to me! And shall I, from any false deference to that conventional voice which proclaims this thing as 'nice,' and that thing as 'not nice,' reject a handicraft which promises me both artistic satisfaction and a competence? No, gentlemen; my claim is a small one,—only a fair day's wage for a fair day's work. But I can accept nothing less, nor consent to forgo my rights, even for any contingent remainder of possible cousinly favour!"

KENNETH GRAHAME

There was a touch of scorn in her fine contralto voice as she finished speaking; the Mayor himself beamed approval. He was not wealthy, and had a large family of daughters; so Jeanne's sentiments seemed to him entirely right and laudable.

"Well, gentlemen," he began briskly, "then all we've got to do, is to—"

"Beg pardon, your worship," put in Master Robinet, the tanner, who had been sitting with a petrified, Bill-the-Lizard sort of expression during the speechifying: "but are we to understand as how this here young lady is going to be the public executioner of this here town?"

"Really, neighbour Robinet," said the Mayor, somewhat pettishly, "you've got ears like the rest of us, I suppose; and you know the contents of the deed; and you've had my assurance that it's—er—quite in order; and as it's getting towards lunch-time—"

"But it's unheard of," protested honest Robinet. "There hasn't ever been no such thing—leastways not as I've heard tell."

"Well, well, well," said the Mayor, "everything must have a beginning, I suppose. Times are different now, you know. There's the march of intellect, and—er—all that sort of thing. We must advance with the times—don't you see, Robinet?—advance with the times!"

"Well, I'm—" began the tanner.

But no one heard, on this occasion, the tanner's opinion as to his condition, physical or spiritual; for the clear contralto cut short his obtestations.

"If there's really nothing more to be said, Mr. Mayor," she remarked, "I need not trespass longer on your valuable time. I propose to take up the duties of my office to-morrow morning, at the usual hour. The salary will, I assume, be reckoned from the same date; and I shall make the customary quarterly application for such additional emoluments as may have accrued to me during that period. You see I am familiar with the routine. Good-morning, gentlemen!" And as she passed from the Council chamber, her small head held erect, even the tanner felt that she took with her a large portion of the May sunshine which was condescending that morning to gild their deliberations.

II

One evening, a few weeks later, Jeanne was taking a stroll on the ramparts of the town, a favourite and customary walk of hers when business cares were over. The pleasant expanse of country that lay spread beneath her—the rich sunset, the gleaming, sinuous river, and the noble old château that dominated both town and pasture from its adjacent height—all served to stir and bring out in her those poetic impulses which had lain dormant during the working day; while the cool evening breeze smoothed out and obliterated any little jars or worries which might have ensued during the practice of a profession in which she was still something of a novice. This evening she felt fairly happy and content. True, business was rather brisk, and her days had been fully occupied; but this mattered little so long as her modest efforts were appreciated, and she was now really beginning to feel that, with practice, her work was creditably and artistically done. In a satisfied, somewhat dreamy mood, she was drinking in the various sweet influences of the evening, when she perceived her cousin approaching.

"Good-evening, Enguerrand," cried Jeanne pleasantly; she was thinking that since she had begun to work for her living she had hardly seen him—and they used to be such good friends. Could anything have occurred to offend him?

Enguerrand drew near somewhat moodily, but could not help allowing his expression to relax at sight of her fair young face, set in its framework of rich brown hair, wherein the sunset seemed to have tangled itself and to cling, reluctant to leave it.

"Sit down, Enguerrand," continued Jeanne, "and tell me what you've been doing this long time. Been very busy, and winning forensic fame and gold?"

"Well, not exactly," said Enguerrand, moody once more. "The fact is, there's so much interest required nowadays at the courts that unassisted talent never gets a chance. And you, Jeanne?"

"Oh, I don't complain," answered Jeanne lightly. "Of course, it's fair-time just now, you know, and we're always busy then. But work will be lighter soon, and then I'll get a day off, and we'll have a delightful ramble and picnic in the woods, as we used to do when we were children. What fun we had in those old days, Enguerrand! Do you remember when we were quite little tots, and used to play at executions in the back-garden, and you were a bandit and a buccaneer, and all sorts of dreadful things, and I used to chop off your head with a paper-knife? How pleased dear father used to be!"

"Jeanne," said Enguerrand, with some hesitation, "you've touched upon the very subject that I came to speak to you about. Do you know, dear, I can't help feeling—it may be unreasonable, but still the feeling is there—that the profession you have adopted is not quite—is just a little—"

"Now, Enguerrand!" said Jeanne, an angry flash sparkling in her eyes. She was a little touchy on this subject, the word she most affected to despise being also the one she most dreaded,—the adjective "unladylike."

"Don't misunderstand me, Jeanne," went on Enguerrand imploringly: "you may naturally think that, because I should have succeeded to the post, with its income and perquisites, had you relinquished your claim, there is therefore some personal feeling in my remonstrances. Believe me, it is not so. My own interests do not weigh with me for a moment. It is on your account, Jeanne, and yours alone, that I ask you to consider whether the higher æsthetic qualities, which I know you possess, may not become cramped and thwarted by 'the trivial round, the common task,' which you have lightly undertaken. However laudable a professional life may be, one always feels that with a delicate organism such as woman, some of the bloom may possibly get rubbed off the peach."

"Well, Enguerrand," said Jeanne, composing herself with an effort, though her lips were set hard, "I will do you the justice to believe that personal advantage does not influence you, and I will try to reason calmly with you, and convince you that you are simply hide-bound by old-world prejudice. Now, take yourself, for instance, who come here to instruct me: what does *your* profession amount to, when all's said and done? A mass of lies, quibbles, dodges, and tricks, that would make any self-respecting executioner blush! And even with the dirty weapons at your command, you make but a poor show of it. There was that wretched fellow you defended only two days ago. (I was in court during the trial—professional interest, you know.) Well, he had his regular *alibi* all ready, as clear as clear could be; only you must needs go and mess and bungle the thing up, so that, just as I expected all along, he was passed on to me for treatment in due course. You may like to have his opinion—that of a shrewd, though unlettered person. 'It's a real pleasure, miss,' he said, 'to be handled by you. You *knows* your work, and you *does* your work—though p'raps I ses it as shouldn't. If that blooming fool of a mouthpiece of mine'—he was referring to you, dear, in your capacity of advocate—'had known his business half as well as you do yours, I shouldn't a bin here now!' And you know, Enguerrand, he was perfectly right."

"Well, perhaps he was," admitted Enguerrand. "You see, I had been working at a sonnet the night before, and I couldn't get the rhymes right, and they would keep coming into my head in court and mixing themselves up with the *alibi*. But look here, Jeanne, when you saw I was going off the track, you might have given me a friendly hint, you know—for old times' sake, if not for the prisoner's!"

"I daresay," replied Jeanne calmly: "perhaps you'll tell me why I should sacrifice my interests because you're unable to look after yours. You forget that I receive a bonus, over and above my salary, upon each exercise of my functions!"

"True," said Enguerrand gloomily: "I did forget that. I wish I had your business aptitudes, Jeanne."

"I daresay you do," remarked Jeanne. "But you see, dear, how all your arguments fall to the ground. You mistake a prepossession for a logical base. Now if I had gone, like that Clairette you used to dangle after, and been waiting-woman to some grand lady in a château,—a thin-blooded compound of drudge and sycophant,—then, I suppose, you'd have been perfectly satisfied. So feminine! So genteel!"

"She's not a bad sort of girl, little Claire," said Enguerrand reflectively (thereby angering Jeanne afresh): "but putting her aside,—of course you could always beat me at argument, Jeanne; you'd have made a much better lawyer than I. But you know, dear, how much I care about you; and I did hope that on that account even a prejudice, however unreasonable, might have some little weight. And I'm not alone, let me tell you, in my views. There was a fellow in court only to-day, who was saying that yours was only a *succès d'estime*, and that woman, as a naturally talkative and hopelessly unpunctual animal, could never be more than a clever amateur in the profession you have chosen."

"That will do, Enguerrand," said Jeanne proudly; "it seems that when argument fails, you can stoop so low as to insult me through my sex. You men are all alike,—steeped in brutish masculine prejudice. Now go away, and don't mention the subject to me again till you're quite reasonable and nice."

III

Jeanne passed a somewhat restless night after her small scene with her cousin, waking depressed and unrefreshed. Though she had carried matters with so high a hand, and had scored so distinctly all around, she had been more agitated than she had cared to show. She liked Enguerrand; and more especially did she like his admiration for her; and that chance allusion to Clairette contained possibilities that were alarming. In embracing a professional career, she had never thought for a moment that it could militate against that due share of admiration to which, as a girl, she was justly entitled; and Enguerrand's views seemed this morning all the more narrow and inexcusable. She rose languidly, and as soon as she was dressed sent off a little note to the Mayor, saying that she had a nervous headache and felt out of sorts, and begging to be excused from attendance on that day; and the missive reached the Mayor just as he was taking his usual place at the head of the Board.

"Dear, dear!" said the kind-hearted old man, as soon as he had read the letter to his fellow-councilmen: "I'm very sorry. Poor girl! Here, one of you fellows, just run round and tell the gaoler there won't be any business to-day. Jeanne's seedy. It's put off till to-morrow. And now, gentlemen, the agenda—"

"Really, your worship," exploded Robinet, "this is simply ridiculous!"

"Upon my word, Robinet," said the Mayor, "I don't know what's the matter with you. Here's a poor girl unwell,—and a more hard-working girl isn't in the town,—and instead of sympathising with her, and saying you're sorry, you call it ridiculous! Suppose you had a headache yourself! You wouldn't like—"

"But it *is* ridiculous," maintained the tanner stoutly. "Who ever heard of an executioner having a nervous headache? There's no precedent for it. And 'out of sorts,' too! Suppose the criminals said they were out of sorts, and didn't feel up to being executed?"

"Well, suppose they did," replied the Mayor, "we'd try and meet them half-way, I daresay. They'd have to be executed some time or other, you know. Why on earth are you so captious about trifles? The prisoners won't mind, and *I* don't mind: nobody's inconvenienced, and everybody's happy!"

"You're right there, Mr. Mayor," put in another councilman. "This executing business used to give the town a lot of trouble and bother;

now it's all as easy as kiss-your-hand. Instead of objecting, as they used to do, and wanting to argue the point and kick up a row, the fellows as is told off for execution come skipping along in the morning, like a lot of lambs in May-time. And then the fun there is on the scaffold! The jokes, the back answers, the repartees! And never a word to shock a baby! Why, my little girl, as goes through the market-place every morning—on her way to school, you know—she says to me only yesterday, she says, 'Why, father,' she says, 'it's as good as the play-actors,' she says."

"There again," persisted Robinet; "I object to that too. They ought to show a properer feeling. Playing at mummers is one thing, and being executed is another, and people ought to keep 'em separate. In my father's time, that sort of thing wasn't thought good taste, and I don't hold with new-fangled notions."

"Well, really, neighbour," said the Mayor, "I think you're out of sorts yourself to-day. You must have got out of bed the wrong side this morning. As for a little joke, more or less, we all know a maiden loves a merry jest when she's certain of having the last word! But I'll tell you what I'll do, if it'll please you; I'll go round and see Jeanne myself on my way home, and tell her—quite nicely, you know—that once in a way doesn't matter; but that if she feels her health won't let her keep regular business hours, she mustn't think of going on with anything that's bad for her. Like that, don't you see? And now, gentlemen, let's read the minutes!"

Thus it came about that Jeanne took her usual walk that evening with a ruffled brow and a swelling heart; and her little hand opened and shut angrily as she paced the ramparts. She couldn't stand being found fault with. How could she help having a headache? Those clods of citizens didn't know what a highly strung sensitive organisation was. Absorbed in her reflections, she had taken several turns up and down the grassy footway before she became aware that she was not alone. A youth, of richer dress and more elegant bearing than the general run of the Radegundians, was leaning in an embrasure, watching the graceful figure with evident interest.

"Something has vexed you, fair maiden?" he observed, coming forward deferentially as soon as he perceived he was noticed; "and care sits but awkwardly on that smooth young brow."

"Nay, it is nothing, kind sir," replied Jeanne; "we girls who work for our living must not be too sensitive. My employers have been somewhat exigent, that is all. I did wrong to take it to heart."

"'Tis the way of the bloated capitalist," rejoined the young man lightly, as he turned to walk by her side. "They grind us, they grind us; perhaps some day they will come under your hands in turn, and then you can pay them out. And so you toil and spin, fair lily! And yet, methinks, those delicate hands show little trace of labour?"

"You wrong me, indeed, sir," replied Jeanne merrily. "These hands of mine, that you are so good as to admire, do great execution!"

"I can well believe that your victims are numerous," he replied; "may I be permitted to rank myself among the latest of them?"

"I wish you a better fortune, kind sir," answered Jeanne demurely.

"I can imagine no more delightful one," he replied; "and where do you ply your daily task, fair mistress? Not entirely out of sight and access, I trust?"

"Nay, sir," laughed Jeanne, "I work in the market-place most mornings, and there is no charge for admission; and access is far from difficult. Indeed, some complain—but that is no business of mine. And now I must be wishing you a good-evening. Nay,"—for he would have detained her,—"it is not seemly for an unprotected maiden to tarry in converse with a stranger at this hour. *Au revoir*, sir! If you should happen to be in the market-place any morning—" And she tripped lightly away. The youth, gazing after her retreating figure, confessed himself strangely fascinated by this fair unknown, whose particular employment, by the way, he had forgotten to ask; while Jeanne, as she sped homewards, could not help reflecting that, for style and distinction, this new acquaintance threw into the shade all the Enguerrands and others she had met hitherto—even in the course of business.

IV

The next morning was bright and breezy, and Jeanne was early at her post, feeling quite a different girl. The busy little market-place was full of colour and movement, and the gay patches of flowers and fruit, the strings of fluttering kerchiefs, and the piles of red and yellow pottery, formed an artistic setting to the quiet impressive scaffold which they framed. Jeanne was in short sleeves, according to the etiquette of her office, and her round graceful arms showed snowily against her dark blue skirt and scarlet, tight-fitting bodice. Her assistant looked at her with admiration.

"Hope you're better, miss," he said respectfully. "It was just as well you didn't put yourself out to come yesterday; there was nothing particular to do. Only one fellow, and *he* said he didn't care; anything to oblige a lady!"

"Well, I wish he'd hurry up now, to oblige a lady," said Jeanne, swinging her axe carelessly to and fro: "ten minutes past the hour; I shall have to talk to the Mayor about this."

"It's a pity there ain't a better show this morning," pursued the assistant, as he leant over the rail of the scaffold and spat meditatively into the busy throng below. "They do say as how the young Seigneur arrived at the Château yesterday—him as has been finishing his education in Paris, you know. He's as likely as not to be in the market-place to-day; and if he's disappointed, he may go off to Paris again, which would be a pity, seeing the Château's been empty so long. But he may go to Paris, or anywhere else he's a mind to, he won't see better workmanship than in this here little town!"

"Well, my good Raoul," said Jeanne, colouring slightly at the obvious compliment, "quality, not quantity, is what we aim at here, you know. If a Paris education has been properly assimilated by the Seigneur, he will not fail to make all the necessary allowances. But see, the prison-doors are opening at last!"

They both looked across the little square to the prison, which fronted the scaffold; and sure enough, a small body of men, the Sheriff at their head, was issuing from the building, conveying, or endeavouring to convey, the tardy prisoner to the scaffold. That gentleman, however, seemed to be in a different and less obliging frame of mind from that of the previous day; and at every pace one or other of the guards was shot violently into the middle of the square, propelled by a vigorous kick or blow from the struggling captive. The crowd, unaccustomed of late to such demonstrations of feeling, and resenting the prisoner's want of taste, hooted loudly; but it was not until that ingenious mediæval arrangement known as *la marche aux crapauds* had been brought to bear on him that the reluctant convict could be prevailed upon to present himself before the young lady he had already so unwarrantably detained.

Jeanne's profession had both accustomed her to surprises and taught her the futility of considering her clients as drawn from any one particular class; yet she could hardly help feeling some astonishment on recognising her new acquaintance of the previous evening. That, with all his evident amiability of character, he should come to this end, was not in itself a special subject for wonder; but that he should have been conversing with her on the ramparts at the hour when—after courteously excusing her attendance on the scaffold—he was cooling his heels in prison for another day, seemed hardly to be accounted for, at first sight. Jeanne, however, reflected that the reconciling of apparent contradictions was not included in her official duties.

The Sheriff, wiping his heated brow, now read the formal *procès* delivering over the prisoner to the executioner's hands; "and a nice job we've had to get him here," he added on his own account. And the young man, who had remained perfectly tractable since his arrival, stepped forward and bowed politely.

"Now that we have been properly introduced," said he courteously, "allow me to apologise for any inconvenience you have been put to by my delay. The fault was entirely mine, and these gentlemen are in no way to blame. Had I known whom I was to have the pleasure of meeting, wings could not have conveyed me swiftly enough."

"Do not mention, I pray, the word inconvenience," replied Jeanne, with that timid grace which so well became her. "I only trust that any slight discomfort it may be my duty to cause you before we part will be as easily pardoned. And now—for the morning, alas! advances—any little advice or assistance that I can offer is quite at your service; for the situation is possibly new, and you may have had but little experience."

"Faith! none worth mentioning," said the prisoner gaily. "Treat me as a raw beginner. Though our acquaintance has been but brief, I have the utmost confidence in you."

"Then, sir," said Jeanne, blushing, "suppose I were to assist you in removing this gay doublet, so as to give both of us more freedom and less responsibility?"

"A perquisite of the office?" queried the prisoner with a smile, as he slipped one arm out of its sleeve.

A flush came over Jeanne's fair brow. "That was ungenerous," she said.

"Nay, pardon me, sweet one," said he, laughing: "'twas but a poor jest of mine—in bad taste, I willingly admit."

"I was sure you did not mean to hurt me," she replied kindly, while her fingers were busy in turning back the collar of his shirt. It was composed, she noticed, of the finest point lace; and she could not help a feeling of regret that some slight error—as must, from what she knew, exist somewhere—should compel her to take a course so at variance with her real feelings. Her only comfort was that the youth himself seemed entirely satisfied with his situation. He hummed the last air from Paris during her ministrations, and when she had quite finished, kissed the pretty fingers with a metropolitan grace.

"And now, sir," said Jeanne, "if you will kindly come this way: and please to mind the step—so. Now, if you will have the goodness to kneel here—nay, the sawdust is perfectly clean; you are my first client this morning. On the other side of the block you will find a nick, more or less adapted to the human chin, though a perfect fit cannot, of course, be guaranteed in every case. So! Are you pretty comfortable?"

"A bed of roses," replied the prisoner. "And what a really admirable view one gets of the valley and the river, from just this particular point!"

"Charming, is it not?" replied Jeanne. "I'm so glad you do justice to it. Some of your predecessors have really quite vexed me by their inability to appreciate that view. It's worth coming here to see it. And now, to return to business for one moment,—would you prefer to give the word yourself? Some people do; it's a mere matter of taste. Or will you leave yourself entirely in my hands?"

"Oh, in your fair hands," replied her client, "which I beg you to consider respectfully kissed once more by your faithful servant to command."

Jeanne, blushing rosily, stepped back a pace, moistening her palms as she grasped her axe, when a puffing and blowing behind caused her to turn her head, and she perceived the Mayor hastily ascending the scaffold.

"Hold on a minute, Jeanne, my girl," he gasped. "Don't be in a hurry. There's been some little mistake."

Jeanne drew herself up with dignity. "I'm afraid I don't quite understand you, Mr. Mayor," she replied in freezing accents. "There's been no little mistake on my part that I'm aware of."

"No, no, no," said the Mayor apologetically; "but on somebody else's there has. You see it happened in this way: this here young fellow was going round the town last night; and he'd been dining, I should say, and he was carrying on rather free. I will only say so much in your presence, that he was carrying on decidedly free. So the town-guard happened to come across him, and he was very high and very haughty, he was, and wouldn't give his name nor yet his address—as a gentleman should, you know, when he's been dining and carrying on free. So our fellows just ran him in—and it took the pick of them all their time to do it, too. Well, then, the other chap who was in prison—the gentleman who obliged you yesterday, you know—what does he do but slip out and run away in the middle of all the row and confusion; and very inconsiderate and ungentlemanly it was of him to take advantage of us in that mean way, just when we wanted a little sympathy and forbearance. Well, the Sheriff comes this morning to fetch out his man for execution, and he knows there's only one man to execute, and he sees there's only one man in prison, and it all seems as simple as A B C—he never was much of a mathematician, you know—so he fetches our friend here along, quite gaily. And—and that's how it came about, you see; *hinc illæ lachrymæ*, as the Roman poet has it. So now I shall just give this young fellow a good talking to, and discharge him with a caution; and we sha'n't require you any more to-day, Jeanne, my girl."

"Now, look here, Mr. Mayor," said Jeanne severely, "you utterly fail to grasp the situation in its true light. All these little details may be interesting in themselves, and doubtless the press will take note of them; but they are entirely beside the point. With the muddleheadedness of your officials (which I have frequently remarked upon) I have nothing whatever to do. All I know is, that this young gentleman has been formally handed over to me for execution, with all the necessary legal requirements; and executed he has got to be. When my duty has been performed, you are at liberty to reopen the case if you like; and any 'little mistake' that may have occurred through your stupidity you can then rectify at your leisure. Meantime, you've no *locus standi* here at all; in fact, you've no business whatever lumbering up my scaffold. So shut up and clear out."

"Now, Jeanne, do be reasonable," implored the Mayor. "You women are so precise. You never will make any allowance for the necessary margin of error in things."

"If I were to allow the necessary margin for all *your* errors, Mayor," replied Jeanne coolly, "the edition would have to be a large-paper one, and even then the text would stand a poor chance. And now, if you don't allow me the necessary margin to swing my axe, there may be another 'little mistake'—"

But at this point a hubbub arose at the foot of the scaffold, and Jeanne, leaning over, perceived sundry tall fellows, clad in the livery of the Seigneur, engaged in dispersing the municipal guard by the agency of well-directed kicks, applied with heartiness and anatomical knowledge. A moment later, there strode on to the scaffold, clad in black velvet, and adorned with his gold chain of office, the stately old seneschal of the Château, evidently in a towering passion.

"Now, mark my words, you miserable little bladder-o'-lard," he roared at the Mayor (whose bald head certainly shone provokingly in the morning sun), "see if I don't take this out of your skin presently!" And he passed on to where the youth was still kneeling, apparently quite absorbed in the view.

"My lord," he said firmly though respectfully, "your hair-brained folly really passes all bounds. Have you entirely lost your head?"

"Faith, nearly," said the young man, rising and stretching himself. "Is that you, old Thibault? Ow, what a crick I've got in my neck! But that view of the valley was really delightful!"

"Did you come here simply to admire the view, my lord?" inquired Thibault severely.

"I came because my horse would come," replied the young Seigneur lightly: "that is, these gentlemen here were so pressing; they would not hear of any refusal; and besides, they forgot to mention what my attendance was required in such a hurry for. And when I got here, Thibault, old fellow, and saw that divine creature—nay, a goddess, *dea certé*—so graceful, so modest, so anxious to acquit herself with credit—Well, you know my weakness; I never could bear to disappoint a woman. She had evidently set her heart on taking my head; and as she had my heart already—"

"I think, my lord," said Thibault, with some severity, "you had better let me escort you back to the Château. This appears to be hardly a safe place for light-headed and susceptible persons!"

Jeanne, as was natural, had the last word. "Understand me, Mr. Mayor," said she, "these proceedings are entirely irregular. I decline to recognise them, and when the quarter expires I shall claim the usual bonus!"

V

When, an hour or two later, an invitation arrived—courteously worded but significantly backed by an escort of half-a-dozen tall archers—for both Jeanne and the Mayor to attend at the Château without delay, Jeanne for her part received it with neither surprise nor reluctance. She had felt it especially hard that the only two interviews fate had granted her with the one man who had made some impression on her heart should be hampered, the one by considerations of propriety, the other by the conflicting claims of her profession and its duties. On this occasion, now, she would have an excellent chaperon in the Mayor; and, business being over for the day, they could meet and unbend on a common social footing. The Mayor was not at all surprised either, considering what had gone before; but he was exceedingly terrified, and sought some consolation from Jeanne as they proceeded together to the Château. That young lady's remarks, however, could hardly be called exactly comforting.

"I always thought you'd put your foot in it some day, Mayor," she said. "You are so hopelessly wanting in system and method. Really, under the present happy-go-lucky police arrangements, I never know whom I may not be called upon to execute. Between you and my cousin Enguerrand, life is hardly safe in this town. And the worst of it is, that we other officials on the staff have to share in the discredit."

"What do you think they'll do to me, Jeanne?" whimpered the Mayor, perspiring freely.

"Can't say, I'm sure," pursued the candid Jeanne. "Of course, if it's anything in the *rack* line of business, I shall have to superintend the arrangements, and then you can feel sure you're in capable hands. But probably they'll only fine you pretty smartly, give you a month or two in the dungeons, and dismiss you from your post; and you will hardly grudge any slight personal inconvenience resulting from an arrangement so much to the advantage of the town."

This was hardly reassuring, but the Mayor's official reprimand of the previous day still rankled in this unforgiving young person's mind.

On their reaching the Château the Mayor was conducted aside, to be dealt with by Thibault; and from the sounds of agonised protestation and lament which shortly reached Jeanne's ears, it was evident that he was having a *mauvais quart d'heure*. The young lady was shown respectfully into a chamber apart, where she had hardly had time to admire sufficiently the good taste of the furniture and the magnificence of the tapestry with which the walls were hung, when the Seigneur entered and welcomed her with a cordial grace that put her entirely at her ease.

"Your punctuality puts me to shame, fair mistress," he said, "considering how unwarrantably I kept you waiting this morning, and how I tested your patience by my ignorance and awkwardness."

He had changed his dress, and the lace round his neck was even richer than before. Jeanne had always considered one of the chief marks of a well-bred man to be a fine disregard for the amount of his washing-bill; and then with what good taste he referred to recent events—putting himself in the wrong, as a gentleman should!

"Indeed, my lord," she replied modestly, "I was only too anxious to hear from your own lips that you bore me no ill-will for the part forced on me by circumstances in our recent interview. Your lordship has sufficient critical good sense, I feel sure, to distinguish between the woman and the official."

"True, Jeanne," he replied, drawing nearer; "and while I shrink from expressing, in their fulness, all the feelings that the woman inspires in me, I have no hesitation—for I know it will give you pleasure—in acquainting you with the entire artistic satisfaction with which I watched you at your task!"

"But, indeed," said Jeanne, "you did not see me at my best. In fact, I can't help wishing—it's ridiculous, I know, because the thing is hardly practicable—but if I could only have carried my performance quite through, and put the last finishing touches to it, you would not have been judging me now by the mere 'blocking-in' of what promised to be a masterpiece!"

"Yes, I wish it could have been arranged somehow," said the Seigneur, reflectively; "but perhaps it's better as it is. I am content to let the artist remain for the present on trust, if I may only take over, fully paid up, the woman I adore!"

Jeanne felt strangely weak. The official seemed oozing out at her fingers and toes, while the woman's heart beat even more distressingly.

"I have one little question to ask," he murmured (his arm was about her now).

"Do I understand that you still claim your bonus?"

Jeanne felt like water in his strong embrace; but she nerved herself to answer, faintly but firmly, "Yes!"

"Then so do I," he replied, as his lips met hers.

EXECUTIONS CONTINUED TO OCCUR IN St. Radegonde; the Radegundians being conservative and very human. But much of the innocent enjoyment that formerly attended them departed after the fair Châtelaine had ceased to officiate. Enguerrand, on succeeding to the post, wedded Clairette, she being (he was heard to say) a more suitable match in mind and temper than others of whom he would name no names. Rumour had it, that he found his match and something over; while as for temper—and mind (which she gave him in bits). But the domestic trials of high-placed officials have a right to be held sacred. The profession, in spite of his best endeavours, languished nevertheless. Some said that the scaffold lacked its old attraction for criminals of spirit; others, more unkindly, that the headsman was the innocent cause, and that Enguerrand was less fatal in his new sphere than formerly, when practising in the criminal court as advocate for the defence.

A Note About the Author

Kenneth Grahame (1859–1932) was a Scottish author of children's literature. Following the death of his mother at a young age, Grahame was sent to live with his grandmother in Berkshire, England, in a home near the River Thames. Unable to study at Oxford due to financial reasons, Grahame embarked on a career with the Bank of England, eventually retiring to devote himself to writing. An early exposure to nature and wildlife formed a lasting impression on Grahame, who would return to the Thames Valley of his youth throughout his literary career—most notably in his novel *The Wind in the Willows* (1908), which is considered his finest achievement and a masterpiece of children's fiction.

A Note from the Publisher

Spanning many genres, from non-fiction essays to literature classics to children's books and lyric poetry, Mint Edition books showcase the master works of our time in a modern new package. The text is freshly typeset, is clean and easy to read, and features a new note about the author in each volume. Many books also include exclusive new introductory material. Every book boasts a striking new cover, which makes it as appropriate for collecting as it is for gift giving. Mint Edition books are only printed when a reader orders them, so natural resources are not wasted. We're proud that our books are never manufactured in excess and exist only in the exact quantity they need to be read and enjoyed.

bookfinity™

Discover more of your favorite classics with Bookfinity™.

- Track your reading with custom book lists.
- Get great book recommendations for your personalized Reader Type.
- Add reviews for your favorite books.
- AND MUCH MORE!

Visit **bookfinity.com** and take the fun Reader Type quiz to get started.

Enjoy our classic and modern companion pairings!

Classic & Modern